The story of
HAPPY TOOTH
& Sad Tooth

By Ariel Cornwall

Illustrated By Jasmine T. Mills

Once upon a time,

in a mouth **so wide**,

there were **twenty baby**

teeth, that lived inside.

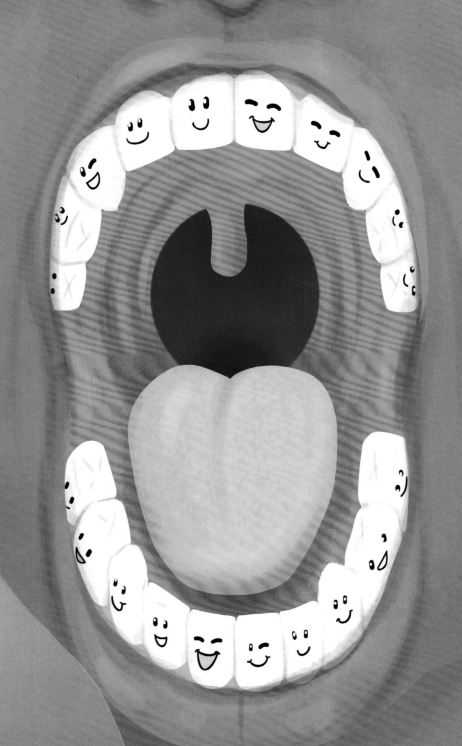

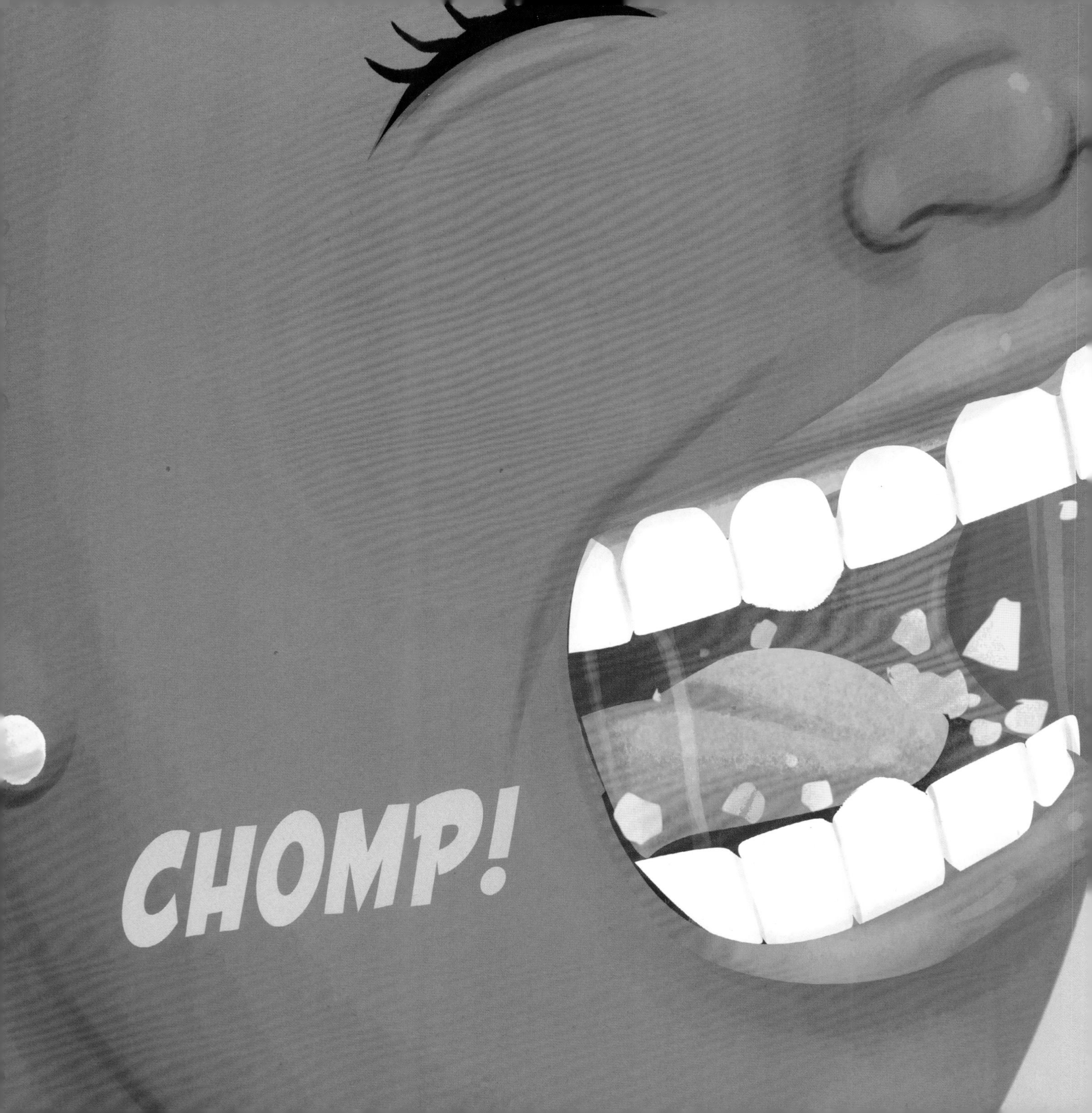
CHOMP!

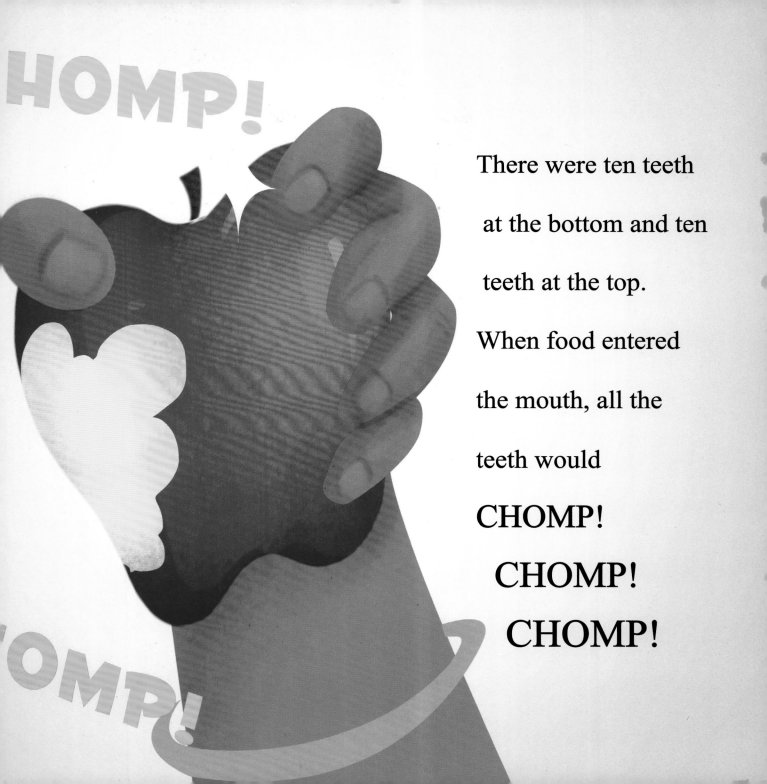

There were ten teeth
at the bottom and ten
teeth at the top.
When food entered
the mouth, all the
teeth would

CHOMP!

CHOMP!

CHOMP!

To keep them healthy, they had to chew healthy food.

Foods like **carrots** and **apples** kept the teeth in a **happy mood.**

After chewing food,
the teeth **loved**
to be visited by
Mrs. Soft Bristle
and **Mr. Flossy.**

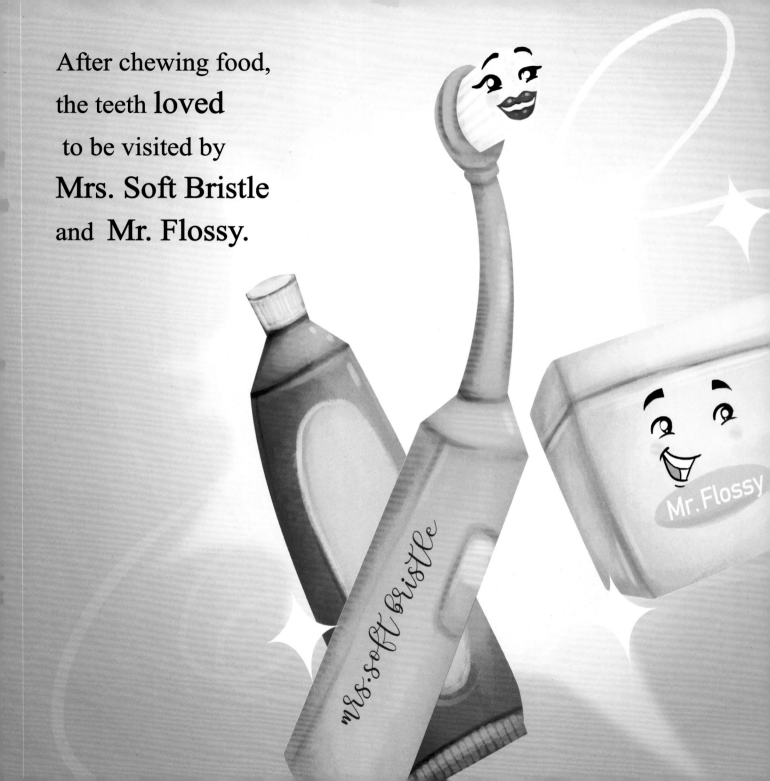

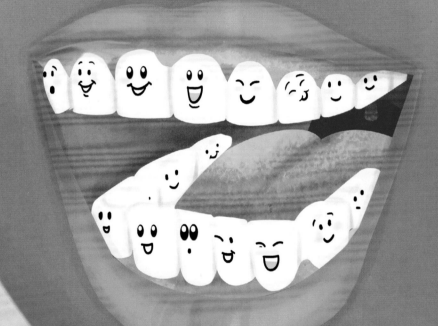

Mr. Flossy would give all the teeth **really good hugs** and Mrs. Soft Bristle would **clean** and **brush** them with **toothpaste suds.**

Oh, how they loved to be **brushed all around** and **flossed in between!** Doing this **twice** a day kept the teeth all **nice and clean.**

They would sing: "I'm a happy tooth because I eat healthy food, I brush and floss twice a day to keep the sugar bugs away!"

Every day, they would sing their happy song because they were healthy and clean.

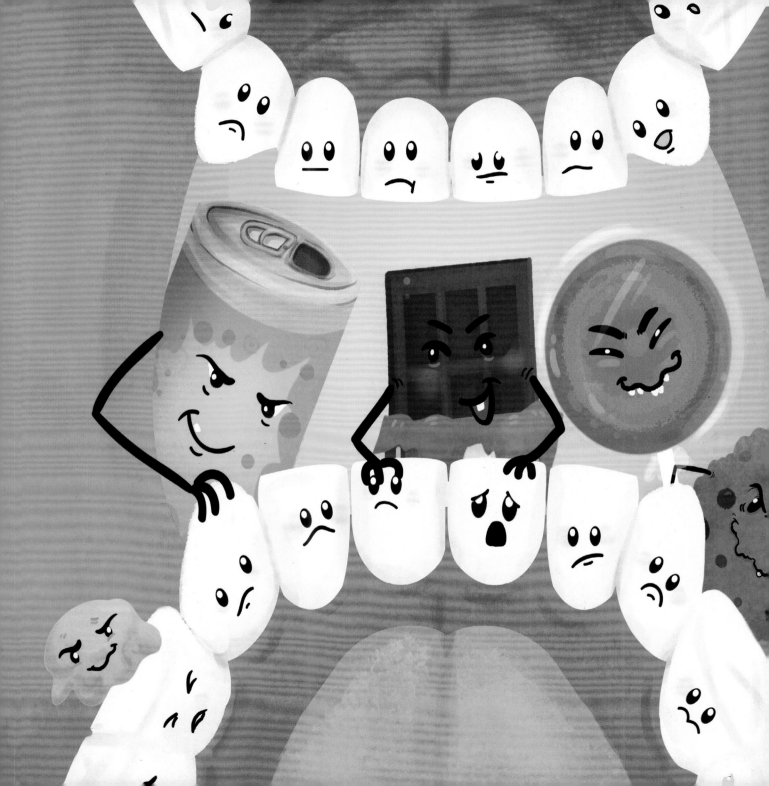

But one day, while they were waiting for **Mrs. Soft Bristle** and **Mr. Flossy** to visit, food entered the mouth, **but there wasn't anything healthy in it!**

There was **candy, cookies,** and even **soda pop too!** There were all kinds of sweet **sticky unhealthy foods!**

For many days, the baby teeth did not see their good friends, Mrs. Soft Bristle and Mr. Flossy.

Oh, No!

Mr. Flossy did not come to give the teeth any hugs!
Mrs. Soft Bristle did not brush them with toothpaste suds!

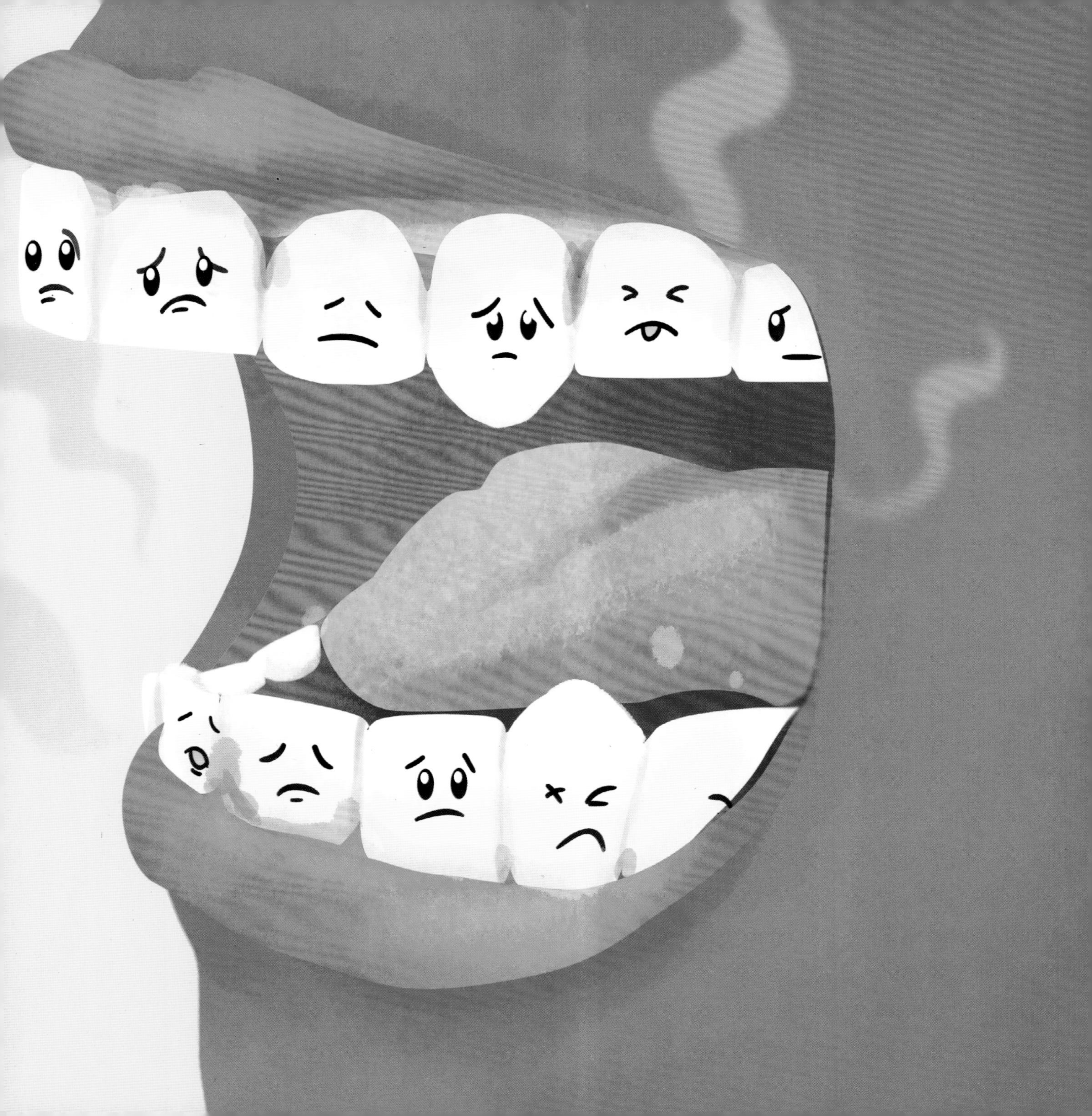

So, the teeth got attacked by the
bad sticky sugar bugs!

The sugar bugs were very mean;
They were a ruthless group.

They would even **potty** on the teeth and leave **sugar poop!**

It didn't take long before some
teeth began to waste away.
They were **turning all black!**
They were **starting to decay!**

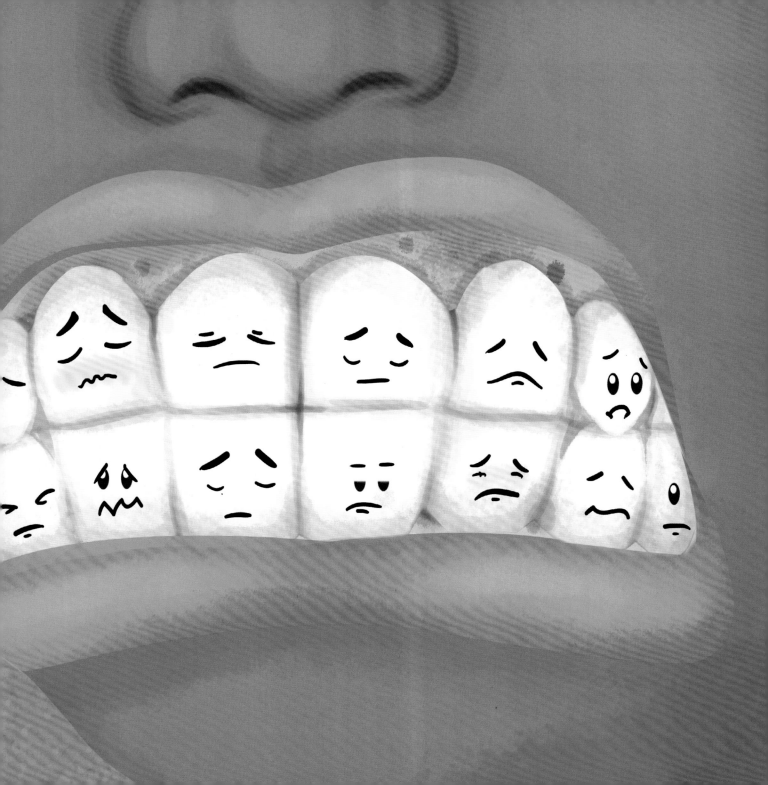

Those teeth would sing: "I'm a sad tooth because I eat bad food, please brush and floss twice a day, to keep the sugar bugs away!"

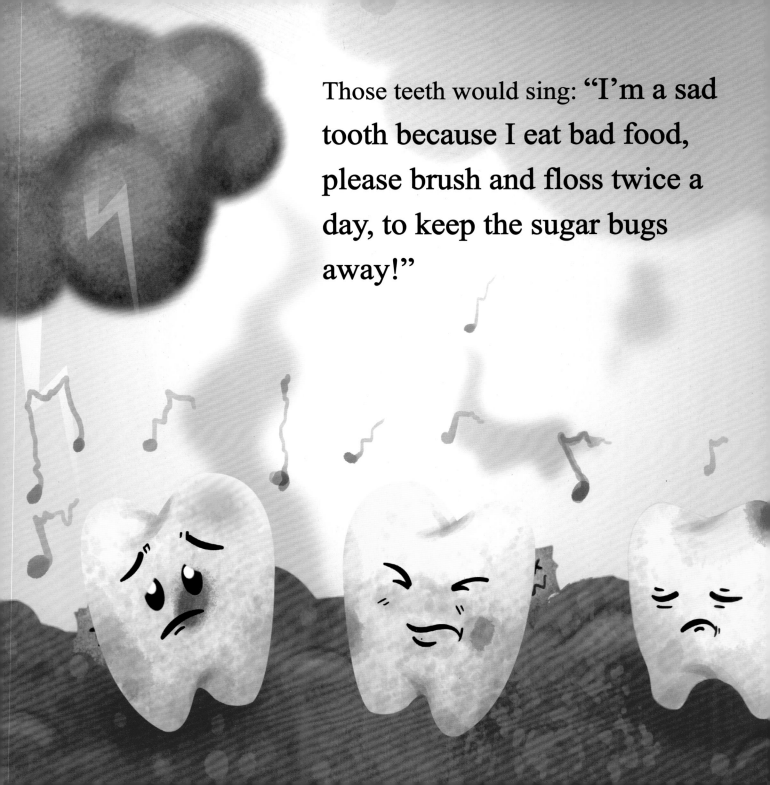

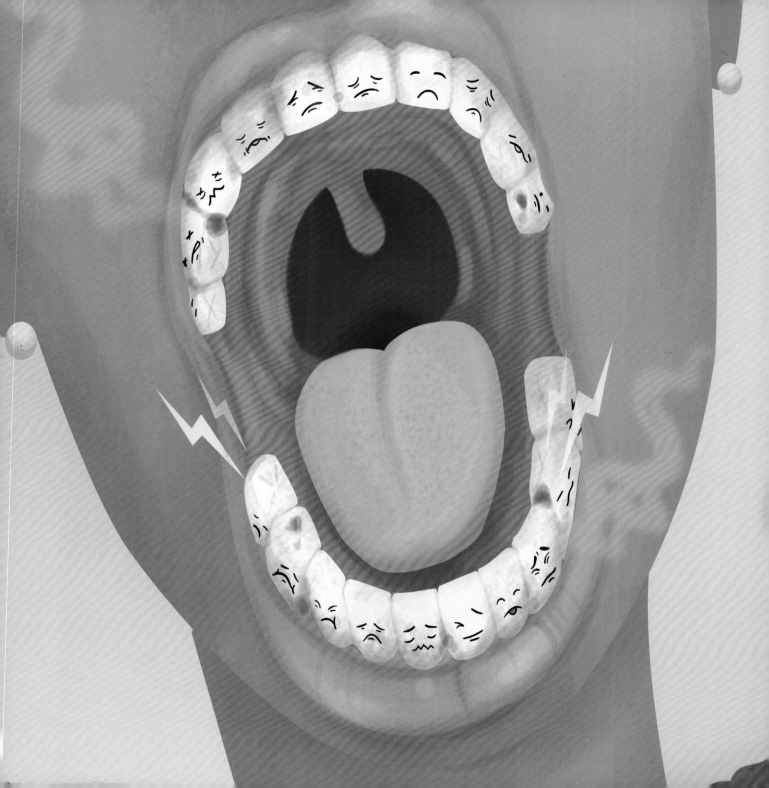

The teeth needed **help** it was time to **stop this!**

They needed **help** from a **really good Dentist!**

Not too long after, the mouth opened,
and to their **surprise**, there was a
very **nice dentist** who **finally**
arrived.

Thank Goodness!

She used her **tools**,

and **removed the decay.**

After she had done that,

all the black went away!

SHE GOT RID OF ALL THE SUGAR BUGS!

Mr. Flossy came back and gave all of the teeth hugs.

And **Mrs. Soft Bristle** brushed all the teeth with toothpaste suds.

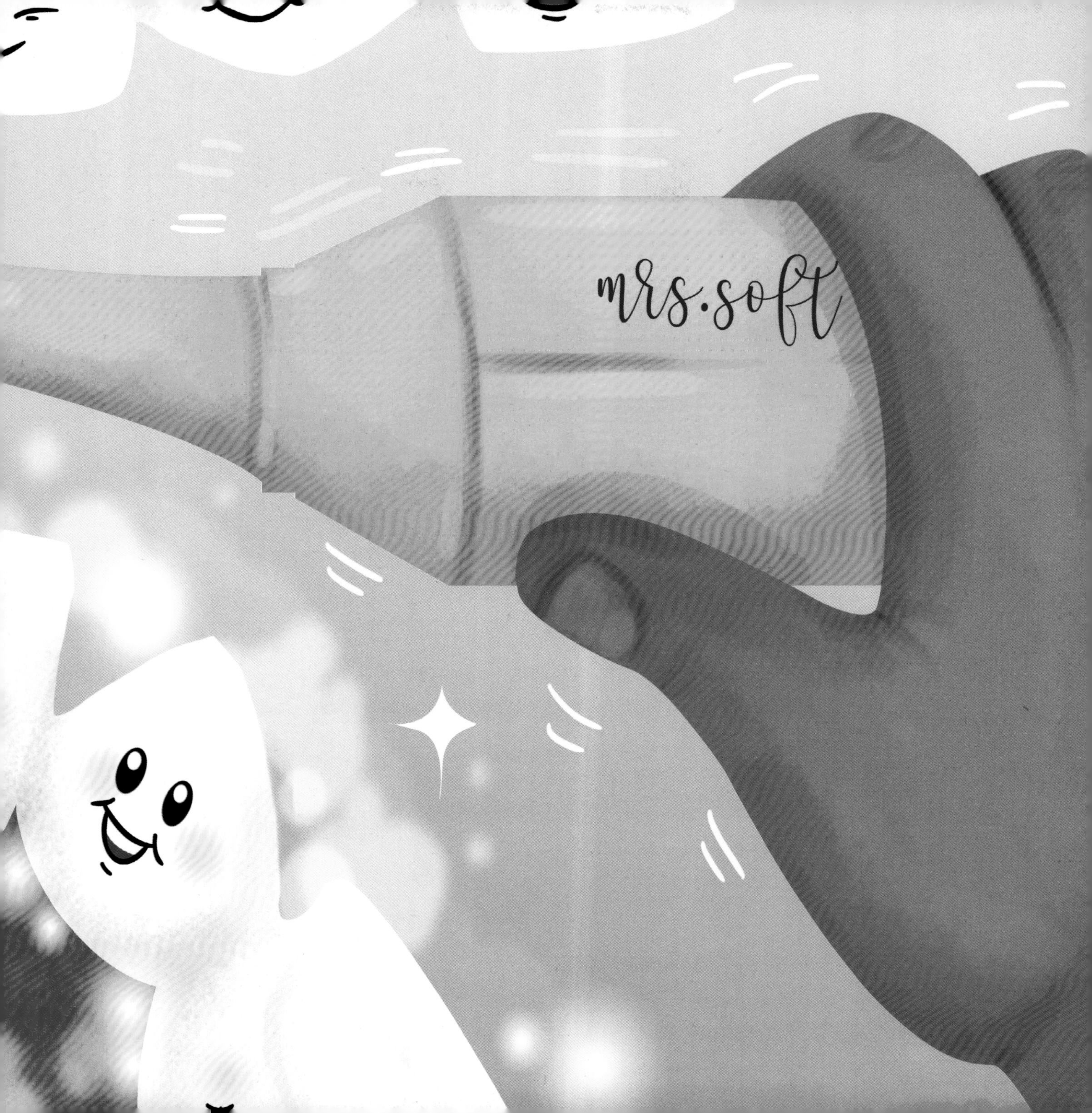
mrs.soft

From that day on, whenever the mouth opened, only **healthy food** was welcomed in.

All twenty teeth lived happily ever after and sang their happy song over and over again.

"I'm a happy tooth because I eat healthy food, I brush and floss twice a day, to keep the sugar bugs away!"

The End

Authors Notes for Parents & Guardians
<u>10 Facts About Tooth Decay</u>

1. Definition of Decay:

Tooth Decay is the destruction of tooth enamel. The result is a hole in the tooth structure.

2. What does decay look like?

It begins by looking like a bright white spot on the teeth called (demineralization). As it progresses, the decay can turn gray, brown or a black color.

3. What is the source of decay?

Decay is caused by foods or drinks containing sugars and starches, bacteria, and poor dental hygiene.

4. How is decay caused?

After consuming food or drink that contains sugar or starches "acidic diet", the bacteria feed on the sugar in your mouth and literally poops acid! The combination of bacteria, food, acid and saliva form a substance called plaque that sticks to the teeth. If not removed by the toothbrush, paste, floss and rinse in an efficient amount of time, the acid continues to corrode the enamel, causing a hole in the tooth structure known as decay.

5. What are the symptoms of tooth decay?

Toothache, tooth sensitivity, bad breath, and/or a bad taste in the mouth.

6. Who is at risk?

Everyone! Because everyone has bacteria in their mouth and has the ability to produce plaque, anyone can be at risk for decay.

7. How is decay diagnosed?

Exam and x-rays from a dentist.

8. How to prevent decay?

Excellent homecare (Brushing, flossing and using a mouth rinse twice daily), eating tooth healthy foods and visiting your dental office for regular checkups and dental cleanings.

9. Can a cavity just go away?

Once tooth enamel is damaged, it cannot be revived. However, weakened enamel can be strengthened to a certain degree by improving its mineral content.

10. What is the treatment if decay occurs?

Early detection is best! Typically, the initial procedure is to allow the dentist to remove the decay and replace the hole with a filling; however, if a cavity gets neglected for too long and increases to a "non-fillable" size, the doctor will have to do more invasive procedures that may include a crown, root canal, or extract the infected tooth all together.

Want to learn more? Visit ArielTheeRDH.com
Follow Ariel Thee Dental Hygienist on Social Media

    @ArielTheeRDH

Acknowledgments:

I am so thankful to have had such extraordinary inspirations in my life. I would like to take the time to honor those who have assisted in my growth as a Dental Hygienist. I could not have gotten as far as I have without your encouragement, tough love, guidance, knowledge, faith and prayers. I am truly grateful!

Family:
Mom, Dad, Greg, Nikoye, Nyanna, Auntie Shay, Uncle Randy "Safewan", Grandpapi, and my Angel in Heaven, Nana.

Atlanta Technical College:
Mrs. Singleton, Mrs. Kemp and the entire DH Program Instructors/ Staff.

My Hygiene Sisters:
"The Flossy Posse"; Ardeita Stallworth, Davina Strozier, Denedria Fletcher, Fantazia Bell, Fateemah McCastle, Jessica Smith, Katelyn Wilson, Knakeba McNeal, Laura Hernendez, Tameron Brown, Antionette Skipper, Yolanda Gowans. And my senior hygienist, Stephanie Blackwell

Thank you all!

Ariel Cornwall, RDH

21989966R00024

Made in the USA
Columbia,SC
04 October 2020